W9-BEZ-433

SHREWSBURY PUBLIC LIBRARY
Shrewsbury, Massachusetts

Gift from Southgate

Assisted Living

The Bed Just So

Retold by JEANNE B. HARDENDORFF

Pictures by Lisl Weil

Four Winds Press   New York

38124000882252
JE
398.2
HARDE

Amazon 2/20/00 #22

PUBLISHED BY FOUR WINDS PRESS

A DIVISION OF SCHOLASTIC MAGAZINES, INC., NEW YORK, N.Y.

TEXT COPYRIGHT © 1975 BY JEANNE B. HARDENDORFF

ILLUSTRATIONS COPYRIGHT © 1975 BY LISL WEIL

ALL RIGHTS RESERVED

PRINTED IN THE UNITED STATES OF AMERICA

LIBRARY OF CONGRESS CATALOG CARD NUMBER: 75-15462

ISBN O-590-07349-4

1 2 3 4 5   80 79 78 77 76

Once there was a tailor who fell asleep
over his work every day.

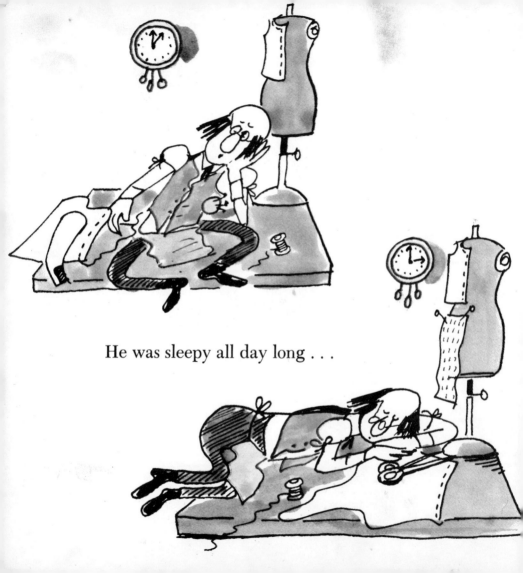

He was sleepy all day long . . .

because he could not get any sleep at night.

Every night, when he began to fall asleep, someone — or some*thing* — pulled the covers off his bed.

And all night long, the tailor thought he heard someone or some*thing* grumbling and complaining and stomping around.

"This can't go on," the tailor said.
And he went to see the Wise Woman.

"I must be witched," he told her.

"No," the Wise Woman said. "If you were witched, your feet would be on backwards. And your hair would be growing upside down. No. Your trouble is that a hudgin has come to stay with you."

"A hudgin!" said the tailor. "What should I do?"

"Make a bed for him," the Wise Woman said. "Then he will leave your bed alone."

So the tailor bought a bed for the hudgin. It was a big, high bed made of oak wood.

"Now," said the tailor, "you have your
bed and I have mine. Let's both have a
good night's sleep."

But as soon as the tailor began to fall asleep,

he heard a voice grumbling and complaining:

> Too high and too hard!
> Too high and too hard!

The next night, the tailor made a low bed of fern and feathers.

But as soon as he began to fall asleep, a voice woke him up, grumbling and complaining:

Too soft and too tickly!
Too soft and too tickly!

Every day the tailor tried a new bed for the hudgin. Every night the voice woke him up, grumbling and complaining.

When the tailor made a bed in the
cupboard, the voice said:

Too dark and too stuffy!
Too dark and too stuffy!

Next he tried a hammock. But the voice said:

Too long and too loose!
Too long and too loose!

The tailor built a cradle. The voice complained:

Too teeter and too totter!
Too teeter and too totter!

The poor tailor could not find a bed to please the hudgin. "I will never get a good night's sleep," thought the tailor. He was very very tired.

But that night he cracked open a walnut to eat after dinner. He looked at the half walnut shell, and it looked to him like a tiny bed.

"Why not?" the tailor thought. "I have tried everything else."

So he lined the walnut shell with cotton and peach down. He put a maple leaf on for a cover. And he put it on the windowsill.

HOPKINTON PUBLIC LIBRARY

Soon he heard a happy humming sound. The tailor looked in the walnut shell. There he saw a small dot, no bigger than a mustard seed.

"Ah, that must be the hudgin," said the tailor. He shut his eyes tight to listen. And he heard a contented voice saying:

Just so. Just so.
I like a bed made just so.

And at last the tailor got a good night's sleep.

4/09

SHREWSBURY PUBLIC LIBRARY

SHREWSBURY, MA 01545

www.shrewsbury-ma.gov/library

Tel: 508-842-0081